The Besties Show and Smell

COLLECT ALL THE BOOKS
IN THE SERIES!

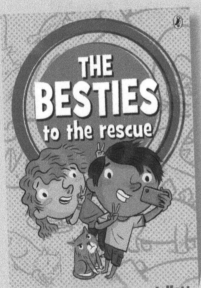

Will the besties
be the BEST
bird-parents
EVER?

Can the besties turn
a very bad school day
into the VERY BEST?

THE BESTIES make a splash

Felice Arena + Tom Jellett

COMING SOON
What if your bestie
is having MORE
FUN at the beach
with someone else?

THE BESTIES party on

Felice Arena + Tom Jellett

COMING SOON
How will the besties' real
party EVER compete
with their AWESOME
practice party?

MEET THE BESTIES!

PUFFIN BOOKS

UK | USA | Canada | Ireland | Australia
India | New Zealand | South Africa | China

Penguin Random House Australia is part of the Penguin Random House
group of companies whose addresses can be found at
global.penguinrandomhouse.com.

First published by Puffin Books, an imprint of
Penguin Random House Australia Pty Ltd, in 2020

Printed and bound in Australia by Griffin Press, an accredited
ISO AS/NZS 14001 Environmental Management Systems printer

 A catalogue record for this
book is available from the
NATIONAL
LIBRARY National Library of Australia
OF AUSTRALIA

ISBN 978 1 76 089098 8 (Paperback)

Penguin Random House Australia uses papers that are natural and recyclable
products, made from wood grown in sustainable forests. The logging and
manufacture processes are expected to conform to the environmental
regulations of the country of origin.

penguin.com.au

THE BESTIES

show and smell

Felice Arena

ILLUSTRATED BY

Tom Jellett

PUFFIN BOOKS

CHAPTER ONE

Ruby rushed into the classroom. She sat at a table and placed her ukulele on top.

'Ollie!' she called, waving at her best friend. 'Ollie!'

Oliver and Ruby had been besties forever.

'I saved you a seat,' she said, pulling a chair out beside her.

Oliver was drawing as he walked.

'Why are you so excited today, Rubes?' he asked,  without even looking up.

③

'It's Show and Tell!' said Ruby. 'I'm going to play a song on my uke. But, even better, we're going to find out what Zac's talent is.'

Oliver looked over at Zac.

It was Ruby and Zac's
turn for Show and Tell.
It was the last one before
the end of term.

Zac turned and caught
Oliver staring at him.

Ruby laughed.

'Whatever he does, it's going
to be gross. I can't wait!'

Oliver looked at his watch. 'I wonder why Ms Perry's not here yet.'

Suddenly, a booming voice filled the room.

'Good morning. I'm Mr Botham. I'll be filling in for your teacher today.'

9

Ruby quickly shot up her hand. 'Do we still get to do Show and Tell?' she asked.

Mr Botham shook his head.

'You get to do Maths worksheets,' he said. 'Yay.' Ruby felt like crying.

CHAPTER TWO

'This is so unfair,' Ruby
whispered.

'Don't worry, Rubes,'
Oliver said. 'You can play
your song for me at lunch.'

Oliver leant over his notebook and started to draw . . .

(14)

Ruby pulled out her pencil.
She reached over and crossed
out Mr Botham's name.

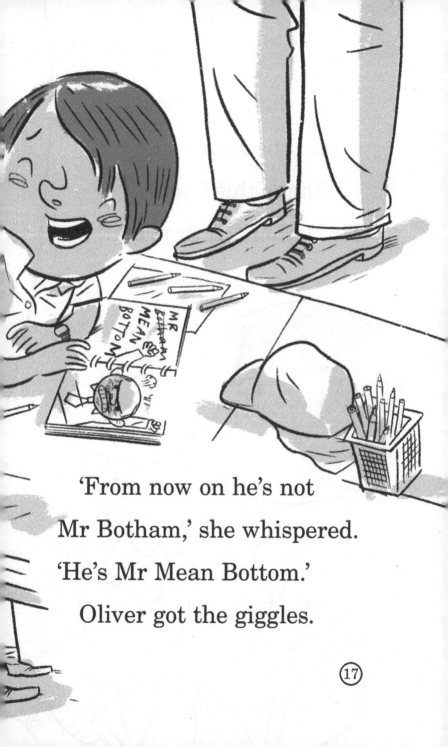

'From now on he's not
Mr Botham,' she whispered.
'He's Mr Mean Bottom.'
Oliver got the giggles.

But then a shadow fell
across the desk.
'What's this?' said
Mr Botham. 'A drawing?'

'Oh no,' said Ruby.

19

CHAPTER THREE

Mr Botham was not happy.
He didn't think Oliver's
drawing was funny at all.

'I can see that you're a
real troublemaker,' he said
to Oliver.

Oliver's face turned bright red. He'd never been in trouble at school before.

MR MEAN BOTTOM

'He's not!' Ruby said.
'Ollie's not a troublemaker.'
'Enough!' Mr Botham
said, screwing up his
stern face.

'I'm separating you two
for the rest of the day,'
he said.

Oliver stood up and moved to where Mr Botham was pointing – a spare seat on his own at the front of the classroom.

'But we always sit together!' cried Ruby. 'We're besties!'

'Too bad,' Mr Botham said and walked away.

Just then an announcement came over the loudspeaker. 'Would Mr Botham please come to the office?'

'Everyone behave, please,' he said. 'I'll be right back.'

Ruby watched the teacher
step out into the corridor . . .

. . . and then out to the
courtyard . . .

... and then he disappeared into the office building.

'Right!' Ruby cried.

Everyone looked up
from their Maths.

'Time for Show and Tell!'
Ruby said. 'I'll go first.'

'Please don't, Rubes,' said
Oliver. 'You're going to get
us into even more trouble.'

'I'm in, too,' said Zac, grinning. 'Let's do it!'

CHAPTER FOUR

Ruby grabbed her ukulele and ran to the front of the classroom.

'It'll be fine, Ollie,' she said. 'You keep watch.'

Oliver sighed.

'Hello, everyone,' Ruby said. 'Here's a little song I wrote about the greatest activity of the week – Show and Tell!'

Strumming to the beat, she sang, 'Dance and sing. Gotta do your thing. Swing your hips like you are the Queen of Cool . . .'

Oliver usually loved watching Ruby play. But today it just made him feel nervous.

The whole class clapped
when Ruby finished.

Oliver felt swirly in
his stomach. What if
Mr Botham caught
them?

Ruby gave a big bow.
Zac clapped the loudest
of all. 'My turn!' he said.

'Hello, everyone!' Zac said in a loud and proud voice.

'The only thing better than Show and Tell is Show and Smell. Today I'm going to teach you all to make a fart noise with your armpit!'

The whole class laughed
and clapped. Everyone gave
it a go!

BRRRP!

BRRRP!

41

Soon everyone could
make a rude noise!

'This is the best Show
and Tell ever,'
cried Ruby.

Oliver ran to the corridor window and looked out.

Mr Botham was on his way back!

CHAPTER FIVE

'Be quiet, everyone,' Oliver said. 'He's coming!'

PRRRP!

One by one, everyone sat
back down in their seats.
Everyone except for Ruby.

Ruby sat down
just one second before
Mr Botham came in.

CHAPTER SIX

All through class Oliver
didn't look back at Ruby
once.

Even when the bell went
and everyone packed up and
left, Oliver still didn't move.

'Ollie?' Ruby whispered.

Her bestie was mad
at her. It didn't feel like
the best day of the week
anymore.

It felt like the worst.

Ruby knew she had to cheer Oliver up.

She picked up her ukelele and walked down the front.

'What are you doing?' Oliver said.

In her best voice, Ruby sang a brand-new verse of her song.

'We are the besties, the perfect double. And I'm so sorry I got you in trouble. I didn't mean to burst your bubble!'

Oliver started to smile.

Ruby was so relieved she threw her arms around him and gave him a big hug.

'Okay,' he said. 'I forgive you. But don't do it again.'

'Hugging is gross!' said a voice.

It was Zac, running up from behind them.

'But not as gross as this! Wanna see me burp the alphabet?'

'No!' the besties said together.

But it was too late . . .

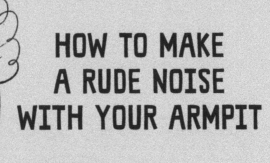

HOW TO MAKE
A RUDE NOISE
WITH YOUR ARMPIT

Step 1.   Make a 'cup' shape with one hand.

Step 2.   Put your hand under your opposite armpit – inside your t-shirt.

Step 3.   Press your cupped hand firmly up against your armpit.

Step 4.   Make sure there is a little space, an air pocket, between your cupped hand and your armpit.

Step 5.   Raise your arm slightly – as if making a 'chicken wing' with your arm.

BRRRRP!

Step 6. Quickly drop your 'wing' back against your body – squeezing out the pocket of air between your cupped hand and your armpit.

Step 7. Who stepped on a duck? Hopefully this will have made a terribly loud and RUDE noise.

Step 8. But, if not, try again. Practice makes perfect . . .

Step 9. *Brrrup!* Was that some thunder from down under? Repeat! Repeat! Repeat!

MY SONG –
SHOW AND TELL

Here are the chords I used to
play this song on the uke:

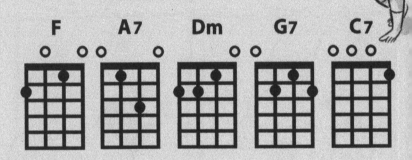

F   **A7**   **Dm**   **G7**   **C7**

    G7   C7
We're the Besties, the perfect double

                    C7
And I'm so sorry I got you in trouble.

F   G7
I didn't mean to burst your bubble

    G7   C7
We're the besties – the perfect double!

F
From Bali to Malawi and the jungle too.
A7
You gotta show the world – it's up to you.
Dm
Dance and sing. Gotta do your thing!
G7   C7
Swing your hips like you are the Queen of Cool!

F
Ding dang dong! Show and tell.
A7
Sing that song, and sing it well.
Dm
Dinga danga dong! Show and tell.
G7   C7   F
Ding, dang, dong. Ring that old school bell.

To hear this song and for all the lyrics,
a full chord sheet and the strumming
patterns go to TheBestiesWorld.com

See you there!

Ruby

THE BESTIES' BEST JOKES!

Why did the teacher go to
the beach?
To test the water!

Which class was the caterpillar
excited about teaching?
Mothematics.

What's the difference between a
teacher and a steam train?
One says, 'Spit out that bubble gum!'
The other says, 'Chew-chew!'

Who's the teacher's best friend
at school?
The princi-PAL!

Why did Ms Perry wear sunglasses?
*Because Ruby and Oliver were
so bright!*

MEET THE SPORTY KIDS!

If you loved meeting the besties you'll love hanging out with the sporty kids . . .

Perfect
for
emerging
readers!

ABOUT FELICE AND TOM

Felice and Tom have done so many books together that they're practically besties! Felice is one of Australia's best-loved children's-book writers, but in his spare time he loves to sing and play the uke. Tom draws the most amazing comics and has done the pictures for so many award-winning and bestselling picture books. They BOTH love burping the alphabet, though!